THE TRAVELLING TREE

written by
Glenn Herring
illustrated by
Kevin Herring

For my children

Eva and William

Rowan the tree lived high up on top of a steep hill. It was cold up there. The wind would blow around his branches and knock off his lovely leaves.

Birds did not come to visit him like some of the other trees he knew.

The strong breeze put them off.

He wanted to have a chat and talk about all
the wonderful places that the birds had visited.

Rowan desperately wanted a change of scenery.

Although the views were fantastic from
the hillside where he lived,
he was fed up with being cold all the time.

He decided to take a walk
to see if there was a
nicer place for him to sit
and chat
with a **sparrow**,
a **robin**,
or maybe even a **pigeon**!

Rowan wandered down the hill,
across a marsh
and into a dark wood.

There were lots of trees
far bigger than him,
with thicker,
uglier barks.

They seemed to ignore him
as he passed them by,
turning their noses up
as Rowan walked
far below them.

He felt very little.

He stopped by one tree and asked,

"Excuse me, do birds visit you here?"

"BIRDS?" snorted the tall tree, "BIRDS?"

"We have mice and we have bugs and we have worms.

Why would we want to talk to birds?"

"YUCK!" thought Rowan,
but politely replied,
"Ah yes, why would you want to
talk to birds with lovely animals
such as bugs and worms?"

Rowan decided that he did not
like the woods.
It wasn't very friendly
and he didn't like the thought
of mice and bugs.

He found a path out and
carried onwards on his journey.
The sun was out and
Rowan liked the feel of the warmth
cuddling him around his branches
like a cosy blanket.

It was much nicer than the
cold breeze that he was
used to up on his hill.

After a while, Rowan came to an orchard.

He liked the way all the trees were smartly lined up in rows.

These trees were a similar size to him, so maybe he could meet some
other trees, just like him. Rowan stood at the end of one
of the rows and stuck his branches out as far as he could.

The tree next to him was a very old lady who turned and smiled.

Rowan smiled back,

"Hello, I'm Rowan. Do birds come to visit you here?"

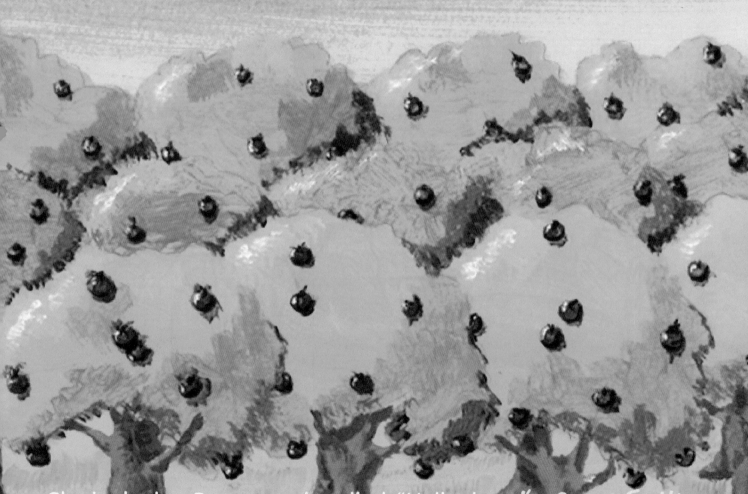

She looked at Rowan and replied, "Hello dear, I'm Granny Smith.
We do get birds, but the farmer chases them off with his broom.
They eat our lovely apples, you see."

This news made Rowan sad. He didn't even know what an apple was or why birds loved to eat them. After a few minutes, a funny looking creature started to move in amongst the orchard trees. It had a red face, two beady little eyes and a pointy thing coming out the middle of its face. It walked slowly and had something weird on top of its head.

"What's that?" asked Rowan.

"That is the farmer," explained Granny Smith.

Rowan had seen a few of these creatures from
afar before, but never up close.
He certainly didn't know that they
were called farmers.

The farmer was very strange indeed.
He kept picking the fruit from all the other
trees and putting them into a bucket.

Rowan didn't want to lose his lovely red berries,
so he quickly ran away, out of the orchard.

Rowan was upset.
He had liked the orchard,
but he certainly didn't want to stay in a place
where a funny creature would tickle his leaves
and steal his nice berries.

Rowan strolled on
until he reached
the seaside.

He looked at the
seagulls hovering
above and he said
to himself,
"I bet they
have some good
stories, maybe
I'll stay here and
talk to them."

He wriggled and wedged himself into the sand
and watched the gulls circle over the ocean,
looking for some fish for their supper.

"**HELLO!**" he yelled, but the seagulls
were too far away to hear him.
"They'll come over at some point," Rowan
thought to himself, "I'll talk to them then."

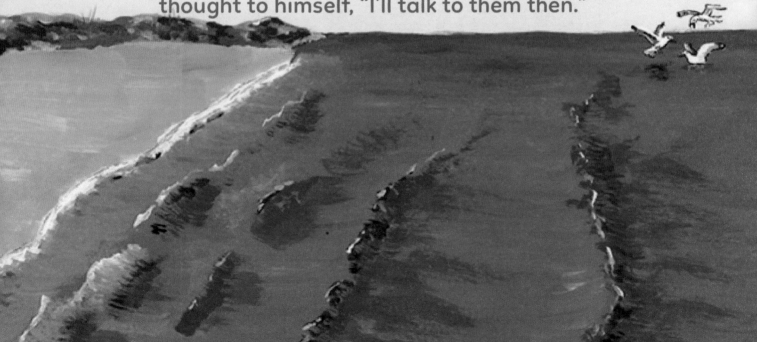

The gulls had been fishing for quite
some time, when suddenly,
Rowan felt a wet tingling in his roots.

He looked down to find that
the sea had risen to his trunk.
He was getting very wet!

The seagulls saw this and squawked madly,
as though they were laughing at him.
If these were the only birds at the seaside,
he didn't want to stay.
Rowan pulled himself free
from the sand and water
and trudged back to the dry land.

His search for a new home was not over.

Rowan dawdled along a little path,
looking down to the floor and
kicking stones as he went.

He was starting to wonder
whether he would ever find
a nice new place to live.

"Maybe I should go back
to my old home,"
he pondered sadly.

As he was about to turn around
and head back to his cold,
windy hill,

Rowan saw the most beautiful
yellow field with red poppies
scattered about.

There was a hedgerow and
some other trees that had
birds sat singing
in their branches.

Rowan's face lit up.

He thought it was the perfect home.

He rushed into the field and found a little clearing

at the edge where he could stare at the magnificent scene.

As Rowan sat down, some birds flew straight into his branches

and started to talk to him.

There was a sparrow, a robin AND a pigeon!

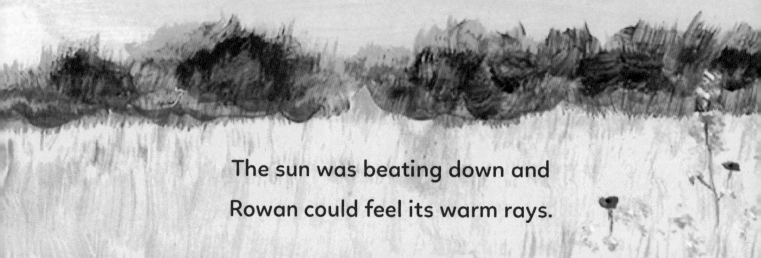

The sun was beating down and

Rowan could feel its warm rays.

The birds started to tell Rowan all
about their adventures and
where they had been, and
Rowan told the birds all about
the journey that he had just made.

From his cold hill,
through the marsh and woods,
into the orchard
with the funny farmer creature,
to the sea that made his roots wet,
along the path and
finally, here, into the
poppy field where he had
made his new friends.

Rowan stretched out his branches and forgot all about his cold, steep hill.

He was home!

Printed in Great Britain
by Amazon